Say It Again, Granny!

for our ancestors who old-talked
for our children to new-talk these proverbs
and for Guyanese folklorist Wordsworth McAndrew
one of our unsung word-preservers.

Say It Again, Granny!

Twenty poems from Caribbean proverbs

John Agard

Illustrated by
Susanna Gretz

LITTLE
MAMMOTH

First published 1986 by The Bodley Head Ltd
Magnet edition first published 1987
Reprinted 1989 by Methuen Children's Books
This edition published 1990 by Little Mammoth
an imprint of Reed Consumer Books Ltd
Michelin House, 81 Fulham Road, London SW3 6RB
and Auckland, Melbourne, Singapore and Toronto

Reprinted 1993
Poems copyright © 1986 John Agard
Illustrations copyright © 1986 Susanna Gretz

ISBN 0 7497 0747 X
A CIP catalogue for this title
is available from the British Library

Printed in Great Britain by
Scotprint Ltd, Musselburgh

Twenty poems from Caribbean proverbs

ROOF CAN FOOL SUN, BUT ROOF CAN'T FOOL RAIN

Drip
drop
roof leaking
sudden rain
bucket time

and I can hear Granny
talking to sheself again

'Well, some people think they so clever
but they can't fool everybody forever.
Roof can fool sun,
but roof can't fool rain.
Why that child taking so long to bring the mop?'

Drip
drop

THE OLDER THE VIOLIN THE SWEETER THE TUNE

Me Granny old
Me Granny wise
stories shine like a moon
from inside she eyes.

Me Granny can dance
Me Granny can sing
but she can't play violin.

Yet she always saying,
'Dih older dih violin
de sweeter de tune.'

Me Granny must be wiser
than the man inside the moon.

ONLY SHOES KNOW WHEN STOCKING GOT HOLE

She said it a hundred times
and she'd say it again

She does say it in sun
and she does say it in rain

'Never stop to roll up yuh stocking
when you running to catch train!'

And she wouldn't stand for back-chat
from young or old

And you can trust her with your secret
she wouldn't tell a soul

But don't ask me why me Granny always saying,
'Only shoes know when stocking got hole.'

DON'T CALL ALLIGATOR
LONG-MOUTH TILL YOU
CROSS RIVER

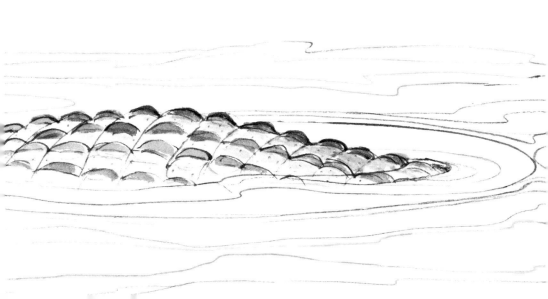

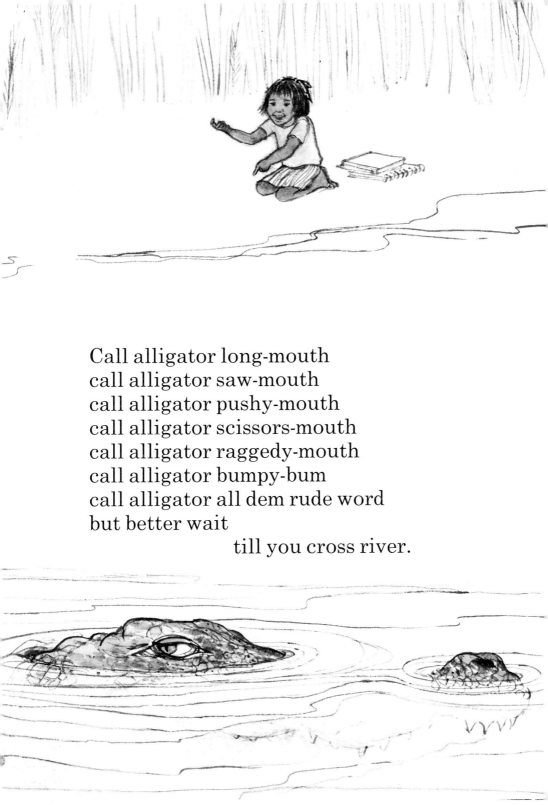

Call alligator long-mouth
call alligator saw-mouth
call alligator pushy-mouth
call alligator scissors-mouth
call alligator raggedy-mouth
call alligator bumpy-bum
call alligator all dem rude word
but better wait
                    till you cross river.

EARLY BIRD DOES CATCH
THE FATTEST WORM

Late again
going to be late again
for school again
and I can't say
I overslept
can't blame it
on the bus
can't blame it
on the train
can't blame it
on the rain
and Granny words
buzzing in my brain
'Early bird does catch the worm,'
and I thinking
Teacher going tell me off
and I wishing
I was a bird
and teacher was a juicy worm.

WHEN BOSS AWAY, JACKASS TAKE HOLIDAY

Yay
Teacher gone out the room
now it's monkey bout time
Quick blow up the balloon!

When the cat's away
the mice will play
that's what Teacher would say.

But me Granny does say,
'When the farmer away,
Jackass take holiday.'

A Jackass is a donkey you know
so when the farmer away
donkey won't have to pull
big heavy dray.

Donkey can eat belly full
Donkey ears can glow
Donkey can even dance disco.

MOUTH OPEN, STORY JUMP OUT

Mouth open
story jump out

I tell you me secret
you let it out

But I don't care
if the world hear
shout it out

Mouth open
story jump out

Besides,
the secret I tell you
wasn't even true
so you can shout
till you blue

So boo
mouth open
story jump out

A THANK-YOU CAN BREAK
NO BONE

When I forget my manners
in the street
or at home

Granny would remind me
'A howdee-do can't hurt you
and a thank-you can break no bone.
Who knows
a please might yet get you
that ice-cream cone.'

Thank you, Granny,
Thank you.

I want another one, please.

IF YOU DON'T HAVE HORSE, THEN RIDE COW

No biscuit!
No biscuit!

What to do?

Forget biscuit
and try some of Granny homemade bread.

No red paint!
No red paint!

What to do?

Forget red paint
and make do with blue.

Granny always telling you:

'Try the best with what you have right now,
If you don't have horse, then ride cow.'

HURRY-HURRY MEK BAD CURRY

People rushing
people pushing
people in a big haste
people in a big speed
not taking their time
like a little seed.

Why all the hurry?
Why all the flurry?
Why all the scurry?

Me Granny does always say,
'Hurry-hurry mek bad curry.'

DON'T COUNT YOUR CHICKENS BEFORE THEY HATCH

I know Granny always saying
when you look forward to something too much
you might be disappointed

But I'm really looking forward
to that new bike,
and when I get that new bike
watch me ride it in the day
watch me ride it in the night
watch me do a wheely in the wind
watch me fancy up a swerve
watch me race and spin.

Nobody going catch me
Nobody
Just watch . . .

Granny would just smile and say,
'Better don't count your chickens
before they hatch.'

But Granny I'm sorry to say
I have a secret to tell

I count me chicks every day
I count them one to ten

so cosy in their egg-house
under warm mother hen.

ONE FINGER CAN'T CATCH FLEA

One finger can wiggle
One finger can tickle
But have you ever seen
a one-finger snap?

One hand can wave
One hand can flap
But have you ever seen
a one-hand clap?

One finger can pat a cat
One finger can stroke a dog
But I'm sure you'll agree
with my Granny
that one finger can't ketch flea.

So let's work together, you and me,
like two hands from one body.

DON'T HANG YUH HAT HIGHER THAN YOU CAN REACH

Me Granny is like avocado pear
me Granny is like fresh sea air
me Granny is like a walk on the beach
and me Granny does say some funny things.

Once when me and Granny went shopping
we passed some expensive hats
in a shop window
and Granny just had one look
and said:

'That's a lovely hat for wearing on the beach
but that kind of money is too much for me
and I never hang mih hat higher than I can reach.'

WHO THE CAP FIT,
LET THEM WEAR IT

If it wasn't you
who tek de chalk
and mark up de wall
juggle with de egg
and mek it fall
then why you didn't answer
when you hear Granny call?

If it wasn't you
who bounce yuh ball
in de goldfish bowl
wipe mud from yuh shoes
all over de floor
and poke yuh finger
straight in de butter

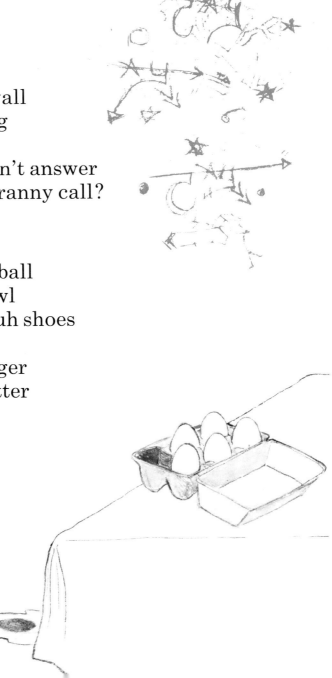

If it wasn't you
then why yuh heart a-flutter?
why yuh voice a-stutter?
and why you look so jumpy
when you stand up in front of Granny?

'Who the cap fit,
let dem wear it.'
That's what Granny does always say
and that she wasn't born yesterday.

WHEN TROUBLE MEET ELEPHANT MONKEY JACKET GO FIT HE

The strong might talk strong
The strong might walk tall
But when the strong fall,
a helping hand
is a helping hand,
even from the small.

If you don't believe me
then just ask me Granny
bout the time
of the famous animal fair
when poor Elephant
didn't have a thing to wear.

You know what Elephant had to do?
And I swear is the truth

Big Elephant had to borrow lil Monkey suit.

FOLLOW-FOLLOW
KILL MONKEY

Just because So-and-So said so
doesn't mean I must say so.

Just because So-and-So did so
doesn't mean I must do so.

Granny does always tell me think for yourself
don't just follow everybody
because follow-follow kill monkey.

Granny even got a song she does sing:

'Everything I do, de monkey would do.
I jump up, monkey jump up too.
I drink gin, monkey drink gin too.
I brush me teeth, monkey brush teeth too.
I eat pepper, monkey eat pepper too.
Hot pepper mek monkey hop like kangaroo.'

BAD DANCER
MUSTN'T BLAME THE FLOOR

You don't have to go to school
to know that bad workers
quarrel with their tools.

So if you make a kite
that's just too heavy
will you blame the wind
for being too light?

So if you make a boat
that just wouldn't float
will you say again
the wind wasn't right?

And if you make a chair
with legs so rickety and thin
when you sit you tumble right in
will you take it with a grin
or will you swear
at the chair
and blame the hammer and nail?

Well, me Granny would just tell you,
'Bad dancer mustn't blame the floor.'

So when music sweet
just move your feet

and don't bother blame the floor.

DRUMMER CAN'T DANCE

I'm always doing
too many things at once

Like brushing my teeth
and trying to sing

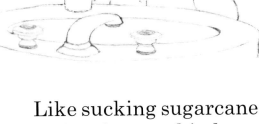

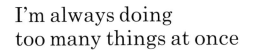

Like sucking sugarcane
and trying to whistle

Like doing homework
and playing scrabble

Granny would ask,
'You ever see somebody dance
and play drum-kit?'

Yes, Granny,
I bet you I do it.
Just give me a drum-kit!

SICKNESS DOES COME ON HORSEBACK, BUT LEAVE ON FOOT

Yesterday I was jumping
yesterday I was hopping
yesterday I was body-popping
yesterday I was doing bumps
on my bike,
just yesterday.

Now today
I got a real bad surprise
the doctor said I have mumps
I wake up with a sicky feeling
and water running from my eyes.
Granny said it must be fever,
the doctor said it's mumps.

Now I can't do bumps,
and Granny said, 'See what I mean,
just yesterday you been so up and about.
Now today the house so quiet.
Sickness does come on horseback,
but leave on foot.
Think about that while you lying in bed.'

I wish the stupid mumps
would jump on a bike
and don't bother come back.

NO RAIN, NO RAINBOW

Suppose today
you're feeling down
your face propping a frown

Suppose today
you're one streak of a shadow
the sky giving you a headache

Tomorrow
you never know
you might wake up
in the peak of a glow.

If you don't get the rain
how can you get the rainbow?

Say it again, Granny,
No rain, no rainbow.

Say it again, Granny,
No rain, no rainbow.